THE WORLD OF
PETER RABBIT
& FRIENDS™
COMPLETE STORY
COLLECTION

THE WORLD OF PETER RABBIT & FRIENDS™
COMPLETE STORY COLLECTION

From the authorized animated series
based on the original tales
BY BEATRIX POTTER™

F. WARNE & CO

FREDERICK WARNE

Published by the Penguin Group
27 Wrights Lane, London W8 5TZ, England
Penguin Books USA Inc., 375 Hudson Street, New York, New York 10014, USA
Penguin Books Australia Ltd, Ringwood, Victoria, Australia
Penguin Books Canada Ltd, 10 Alcorn Avenue, Toronto, Ontario, Canada M4V 3B2
Penguin Books (N.Z.) Ltd, 182-190 Wairau Road, Auckland 10, New Zealand

Penguin Books Ltd, Registered Offices: Harmondsworth, Middlesex, England

This edition first published by Frederick Warne & Co. 1997
3 5 7 9 10 8 6 4 2

This edition copyright © Frederick Warne & Co., 1997
Text copyright © Frederick Warne & Co., 1994, 1996, 1997
Illustrations from *The World of Peter Rabbit and Friends*TM animated television and video
series, a TV Cartoons Ltd production for Frederick Warne & Co., copyright © Frederick
Warne & Co., 1992, 1993, 1994, 1995, 1996

Frederick Warne & Co. is the owner of all rights, copyrights and trademarks in the Beatrix
Potter character names and illustrations.

ISBN 0 7232 4447 2

Printed and bound in Singapore by Imago Publishing Ltd

CONTENTS

THE TALE OF
PETER RABBIT
AND
BENJAMIN BUNNY

Once upon a time there were four little rabbits, and their names were Flopsy, Mopsy, Cotton-tail and Peter.

They lived with their mother in a sandbank, underneath the root of a very big fir-tree.

'Now, then,' said Mrs Rabbit one morning to her children, 'you may go into the fields, or down the lane but don't go into Mr McGregor's garden. Your father had an accident there - he was put in a pie by Mrs McGregor.'

'Run along now and don't get into mischief. I'm going out,' said Mrs Rabbit.

Then she took her basket and umbrella and went through the wood to the baker.

Flopsy, Mopsy and Cotton-tail, who were good little bunnies, went down the lane to gather blackberries.

But Peter, who was very naughty, ran off towards Mr McGregor's garden. On the way he saw his cousin Benjamin.

'Meet me tomorrow - at the big fir tree!' Benjamin whispered.

Peter squeezed under the gate into Mr McGregor's garden.

'Mama will never find out,' he said to himself.

First he ate some lettuces and some French beans; and then he ate some radishes.

'Ooh! My favourite,' he said happily, 'I can't wait to tell Benjamin.'

Peter ate so many radishes that he began to feel rather sick.

'Oh,' he groaned, 'I had better find a little bit of parsley,' and off he went to search for some.

But whom do you think he should meet round the end of a cucumber frame?

'Oh help!' gasped Peter. 'It's Mr McGregor!'

Mr McGregor was planting out young cabbages, but he jumped up and was after Peter in no time, shouting, 'Stop, thief!'

Peter was most dreadfully frightened; he rushed all over the garden, for he had forgotten the way back to the gate. He lost his shoes and ran faster on all fours. Indeed, Peter might have got away altogether if he had not run into a gooseberry net.

'Hurry, Peter, hurry,' urged some friendly sparrows. 'Mr McGregor's coming! Quick, you must keep trying.'

'It's no use,' sobbed Peter trying to struggle free, 'my brass buttons are all caught up.'

Mr McGregor came up with a sieve, which he intended to pop on the top of Peter, but Peter wriggled free leaving his jacket behind him.

He rushed into the toolshed, and jumped into a watering can. It would have been a beautiful thing to hide in if it had not had so much water in it.

'Come on oot, ye wee beastie -
I know you're here somewhere,'
muttered Mr McGregor,
searching for Peter under the
flower pots.

Suddenly, Peter sneezed,
'Kertyschoo!' and
Mr McGregor was after him in
no time.

Peter jumped out of a window
and ran off.

Peter was quite lost. He found a door in a wall; but it was locked and there was no room for a fat little rabbit to squeeze underneath.

He saw a little old mouse carrying peas to her family.

'If you please, Ma'am, could you tell me the way to the gate?' he asked.

'Mmmm,' was all she could mumble in reply.

'Oh, but which way?' asked Peter sadly, and he began to cry.

Presently, Peter came to a pond where a white cat was staring at some goldfish.

'I must be quiet,' he said to himself. 'Cousin Benjamin has warned me about cats.'

And then Peter saw the gate. He ran as fast as he could, slipped under the gate, and was safe at last in the wood outside the garden.

Mr McGregor hung up the little jacket and the shoes for a scarecrow to frighten the blackbirds.

'Where have you been?' asked Peter's mother. 'And where are your clothes? That is the second little jacket and pair of shoes you've lost in a fortnight. You're to go straight to bed without any supper and I will make you some camomile tea.'

But Flopsy, Mopsy and Cotton-tail had bread and milk and blackberries for supper.

The next day Benjamin Bunny was sitting on a bank waiting for Peter.
  'Where has Peter got to?' he wondered, when suddenly he heard the trit trot, trit trot of a pony.
  'Well, what luck! It's Mr and Mrs McGregor going out! I'd better find Peter right away,' he thought and rushed off to find his cousin.

Benjamin found Peter sitting alone,
wrapped only in a red cotton
pocket-handkerchief and looking
very sorry for himself.

'I say!' exclaimed Benjamin. 'You
do look poorly. Who has got your
clothes?'

'The scarecrow in Mr McGregor's
garden,' replied Peter and he told
Benjamin what had happened the
day before.

Benjamin laughed. 'That's what I
came to tell you. Mr McGregor has
gone out in the gig, *and* Mrs
McGregor.'

They made their way to
Mr McGregor's garden and got up
onto the wall. They looked down.
Peter's coat and shoes were plainly
to be seen on the scarecrow, topped
with an old tam-o-shanter of
Mr McGregor's.

'It spoils people's clothes to
squeeze under a gate,' said
Benjamin. 'The *proper* way to get in,
is to climb down a pear tree.'

Little Benjamin said that the first
thing to be done was to get back
Peter's clothes.

There had been rain during the
night; there was water in the shoes
and the coat was somewhat shrunk.

'We can use the handkerchief to carry onions as a present for Aunt,' said Benjamin as they gathered the bundle together.

'Come along Peter,' urged Benjamin.

Peter was not enjoying himself.

Benjamin on the contrary was perfectly at home and ate a lettuce leaf.

Peter did not eat anything and said he should like to go home. Then he dropped half the onions!

But as they turned a corner, Peter and Benjamin stopped suddenly.
  'Gracious, what now, Benjamin?' asked Peter.
  This is what those little rabbits saw round the corner!

'Quick, under here,' whispered Benjamin. 'She's coming towards us.'

Perhaps the cat liked the smell of onions - because she sat down on top of the basket.

'Now what do we do?' sobbed Peter miserably.

'She'll have to go in for her supper soon,' said Benjamin hopefully.

But the cat slept on the basket for *five hours*.

Mrs Rabbit was getting anxious.

'Mr Bouncer, have you seen my son, Peter?
He's been missing all day.'

'Benjamin has taken himself off too,' replied
Benjamin's father. 'Leave it to me, ma'am, I
think I know where the young rascals have got
to. And if I'm right . . .'

'Father!' shouted Benjamin from beneath the basket.

The cat looked up and saw Mr Bouncer prancing along the top of the wall. Mr Bouncer had no opinion whatever of cats and he kicked her into the greenhouse and locked the door.

Mr Bouncer pulled Benjamin from beneath the basket.

'Benjamin first, I think, then Peter . . . Off home with you now.'

Then Mr Bouncer took the handkerchief of onions, and marched those two naughty rabbits all the way home.

When Peter got home his sisters
rushed to greet him.

'Well, at least you've found your
jacket and shoes, Peter,' said
Mrs Rabbit, relieved to see her son
home safely.

'There now my dears,' she added,
'all's well that ends well. But let
that be a lesson to you, Peter.'

THE TALE OF TOM KITTEN AND JEMIMA PUDDLE-DUCK

Once upon a time there were three little kittens, and their names were Mittens, Tom Kitten and Moppet.
  They had dear little coats of their own; and they tumbled about the doorstep and played in the dust.
  'I do wish Mrs Twitchit would keep her kittens in order,' quacked Jemima Puddle-duck.

One day their mother - Mrs
Tabitha Twitchit - expected friends
to tea; so she fetched her kittens
indoors, to wash and dress them
before her visitors arrived.

First she scrubbed their faces and
then she brushed their fur.

'Stay where you are, you two,' she
warned and she dressed Mittens
and Moppet in clean pinafores.

Then it was Tom's turn.

'Goodness me, Tom, I had not realised quite how much you have grown. Oh dear, oh dear!' sighed Mrs Tabitha Twitchit. 'We'll just have to make the best of it.'

She sewed the buttons back on again, and Tom was squeezed into his best suit.

'Now, keep your frocks clean, children,' said Mrs Tabitha Twitchit.
'You must walk on your hind legs. Keep away from the dirty ash-pit. And
from the pigsty - oh, *and* the Puddle-ducks,' she continued.
  Then she let the kittens out into the garden to be out of the way.

'Let's climb up the rockery, and sit on the garden wall,' suggested Moppet eagerly.

Moppet's white tucker fell down into the road. 'Never mind,' she said, 'we can fetch it later. Now, where's Tom?'

'He's still down there,' said Mittens, pointing to the rockery below them.

43

'Come along, Tom, hurry yourself up,' Mittens called.

Tom was all in pieces when he reached the top of the wall; his hat fell off and the rest of his buttons burst.

While Mittens and Moppet tried to pull him together there was a pit pat paddle-pat! and the three Puddle-ducks came along the road. They stopped and stared up at the kittens. Then they caught sight of the kittens' clothes lying at the bottom of the wall!

'Rather fetching, don't you agree, Jemima?' asked Rebeccah, as she tried on Tom's hat.

Mittens laughed so much that she fell off the wall. Moppet and Tom followed her down.

'Come and help me to dress Tom,' said Moppet to Mr Drake Puddle-duck.

But Mr Drake put Tom's clothes on *himself*.

'It is a very fine morning,' he said and he and Jemima and Rebeccah Puddle-duck set off up the road, keeping step - pit pat, paddle pat!

Then Mrs Tabitha Twitchit came down the garden path and saw her kittens on the wall with no clothes on.

'Oh, my goodness,' she gasped, 'just look at you! My friends will arrive any moment and you are not fit to be seen - I am affronted!

'Straight to your room and not one sound do I wish to hear,' she ordered.

When Mrs Tabitha Twitchit's friends arrived I am sorry to say she told them that her kittens were in bed with the measles; which was not true.

'Dear, dear. What a shame. The poor souls,' exclaimed Henrietta.

But the kittens were not in bed; *not* in the least.

At the tea-party, strange noises were heard from above. 'You did say they were poorly, didn't you, Tabitha dear?' asked Cousin Ribby curiously.

As for the Puddle-ducks, they went into a pond. The clothes all came off because there were no buttons, and they have been looking for them ever since.

Indeed, Jemima was no better at finding things than she was at hiding them. She had often tried to hide her eggs, but they were always found and carried off. No-one believed that Jemima had the patience to sit on her eggs.

Poor Jemima became quite desperate.

'I *will* hatch my own eggs, if I have to make a nest right away from the farm,' she said.

So, one fine spring afternoon, Jemima put on her best bonnet and shawl and set off.

Jemima landed in a clearing in the middle of a wood. She began to waddle about in search of a nesting place, when suddenly she was startled to find an elegantly dressed gentleman reading a newspaper.

'Madam, have you lost your way?' he enquired politely.

'Oh, no,' Jemima explained. 'I am trying to find a convenient, dry nesting place so that I may sit on my eggs.'

'Is that so? Indeed! How interesting! As to a nest there is no difficulty: I have a sackful of feathers in my wood-shed,' said the bushy long-tailed gentleman. He opened the door to show Jemima.

'You will be in nobody's way. You may sit there as long as you like,' he assured her.

'Goodness,' thought Jemima, 'I've never seen so many feathers in one place. Very comfortable, though, and perfect for making my nest, so warm . . . so dry.'

The sandy-whiskered gentleman promised to take great care of Jemima's nest until she came back again the next day.

'Nothing I love better than eggs and ducklings. I should be proud to see a fine nestful in my wood-shed. Oh, what would be a finer sight?'

Jemima Puddle-duck came every afternoon, and laid nine eggs in the nest. The foxy gentleman admired them immensely.

  At last Jemima told the gentleman she was ready to sit on her eggs until they hatched.

  'Madam,' he said, 'before you commence your tedious sitting I intend to give you a treat. Let us have a dinner party all to ourselves. May I ask you to bring some herbs from the farm garden to make, er . . . a savoury omelette? I will provide lard for the stuffing . . . I mean, omelette.'

Jemima Puddle-duck was a simpleton; she quite unsuspectingly went round nibbling snippets off all the different sorts of herbs that are used for stuffing roast duck.

'What are you doing with those onions?' asked Kep, the collie dog. 'And where do you go every afternoon by yourself?'

Jemima told him the whole story.

'Now, exactly where is your nest?' enquired Kep suspiciously.

Jemima went up the cart-road for the last time and flew over the wood.

When she arrived the bushy long-tailed gentleman was waiting for her.

'Come into the house just as soon as you've looked at your eggs,' he ordered sharply. Jemima had never heard him speak like that. She felt surprised and uncomfortable.

While Jemima was inside she heard pattering feet round the back of the shed. She became much alarmed. 'Oh, what shall I do?' she worried.

A moment afterwards there were the most awful noises - barking, growls and howls, squealing and groans.

'And I think that is the last we will see of that foxy-whiskered gentleman,' said Kep.

Unfortunately the puppies had gobbled up all of Jemima's eggs before Kep could stop them.

'There, there, Jemima,' comforted Kep, 'I'm afraid it's just in the nature of things - best make our way home to the farmyard, where you belong, my dear.'

Poor Jemima Puddle-duck was escorted home.

Jemima laid some more eggs in June and she was allowed to keep them herself; but only four of them hatched. She said that it was because of her nerves, but she had always been a bad sitter.

THE TALE OF SAMUEL WHISKERS

Once upon a time there was an old cat, called Mrs Tabitha Twitchit, who was an anxious parent. She used to lose her kittens continually, and whenever they were lost they were always in mischief!

On baking day Mrs Tabitha Twitchit
determined to shut her kittens in a
cupboard.

 'And there you stay my two young
rascals, until my baking is finished,'
she said to Moppet and Mittens.

But she could not find Tom.

Tom Kitten did *not* want to be shut in a cupboard, so he looked around for a convenient place to hide and fixed upon the chimney.

Inside the chimney, Tom coughed and choked with the smoke. He began to climb right to the top.

'I cannot go back. If I slipped I might fall in the fire and singe my beautiful tail and my little blue jacket,' he said.

While Mrs Tabitha Twitchit was searching for Tom, Moppet and Mittens pushed open the cupboard door. They went straight to the dough which was set to rise in a pan in front of the fire.

'Shall we make dear little muffins?' said Mittens to Moppet.

But just at that moment, somebody knocked at the door, and a voice called out: 'Tabitha! Are you at home, Tabitha?'

'Oh, come in Cousin Ribby. I'm in sad trouble. I've lost my dear son Thomas. I'm afraid the rats have got him,' sobbed Mrs Tabitha Twitchit. 'And now Moppet and Mittens are gone too. What it is to have an unruly family,' she wailed.

'Well Cousin, we shan't find any of them standing here,' said Ribby firmly.
'I'm not afraid of rats. I'll help you find Tom - and whip him too. Now,
just where would a naughty kitten hide?'

Meanwhile, up the chimney Tom
Kitten was getting very frightened!
It was confusing in the dark, and he
felt quite lost.

All at once he fell head over heels down a hole and landed on a heap of very dirty rags.

'What a peculiar smell,' said Tom Kitten to himself. 'It's something like a mouse . . . only dreadfully strong . . . Oh!' he gasped suddenly.

Opposite to him - as far away as he could sit - was an enormous rat.

'What do you mean by tumbling into my bed all covered with smuts?' asked the rat (whose name was Samuel Whiskers).

'Please sir, the chimney wants sweeping,' said poor Tom Kitten miserably.

'Anna Maria! Anna Maria!' Samuel Whiskers called.
   There was a pattering noise and an old woman rat poked her head
round a rafter.

'What have we here, Samuel?' she asked. 'A tasty morsel indeed!' She rushed upon Tom and before he knew what was happening, he was rolled up in a bundle, and tied with string in very tight knots.

'Anna Maria,' said the old man rat,
'make me a kitten dumpling
roly-poly pudding for my dinner.'

'Hmm . . . it requires dough and a pat of butter and a rolling-pin,'
said Anna Maria.
  The two rats consulted together for a few minutes and then went away.

Samuel Whiskers went boldly down the front staircase to the dairy to get the butter.

He made a second journey for the rolling-pin, which he pushed in front of him with his paws.

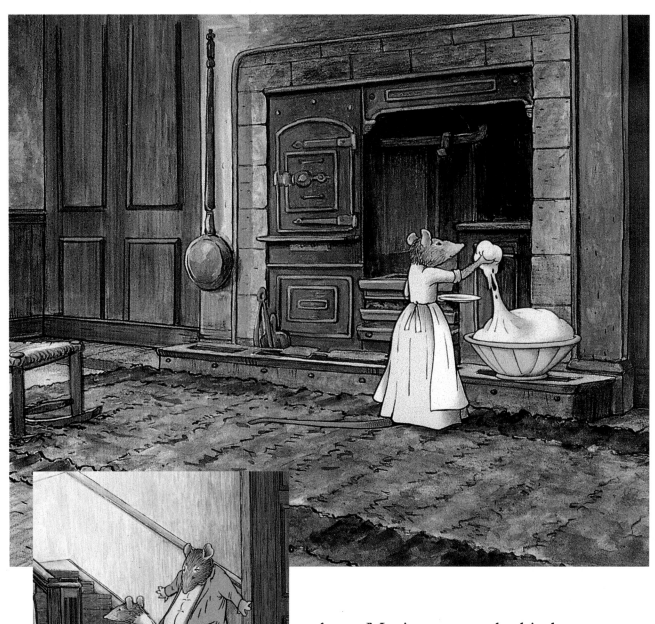

Anna Maria went to the kitchen to
steal the dough. She borrowed a
small saucer, and scooped up the
dough with her paws.

'He is rather a large kitten for his
age,' she muttered, as she scooped
up another pawful.

83

Presently the rats came back and set to work to make Tom Kitten into a dumpling. First they smeared him with butter, and then they rolled him in the dough.

Ribby and Mrs Tabitha Twitchit
heard a curious roly-poly noise
under the attic floor, but there was
nothing to be seen so they returned
to the kitchen. Ribby found
Moppet hiding in a flour barrel.
'Moppet!' scolded Mrs Twitchit.
'But mother,' cried Moppet,
'there's been an old woman rat in
the kitchen and she's stolen some
of the dough!'

Mittens was found in the dairy, hiding in an empty jar.

'There's been an old man rat in the dairy, mother. He's stolen a pat of butter and a rolling-pin!' Mittens cried.

'Oh my poor son, Thomas!' exclaimed Tabitha, wringing her paws.

Ribby and Mrs Tabitha Twitchit rushed upstairs. Sure enough, the roly-poly noise was still going on quite distinctly under the attic floor.

'Oh my goodness, this is serious, Cousin Tabitha,' said Ribby. 'We must send for John Joiner at once, with a saw.'

And what was happening to Tom Kitten? All this time, the two rats had
been hard at work.

'Will not the string be very indigestible, Anna Maria?' inquired Samuel
Whiskers.

'No, no, no. It is of no consequence,' she replied before turning to Tom.
'I do wish you would stop moving your head about. It disarranges the
dough so.'

'Oh, Mr Joiner, this way,' said
Cousin Ribby. 'We can hear the
strangest sounds . . . I dread to
think! Come along, follow me
quickly now.'

'I do *not* think it will be a good pudding,' said Samuel Whiskers, looking at Tom Kitten. 'It smells sooty.'

Anna Maria was about to argue the point, when they heard noises up above - the rasping of a saw, and the noise of a little dog, scratching and yelping!

'We are discovered and interrupted, Anna Maria. Let us collect our property (and other people's) and depart at once. I fear that we shall be obliged to leave this pudding, but I am persuaded that the knots would have proved indigestible,' said Samuel Whiskers.

So it happened that by the time
John Joiner had got the plank up
there was nobody under the
floor except the rolling-pin and
Tom Kitten in a very dirty
dumpling!

Samuel Whiskers and Anna Maria found a wheelbarrow belonging to Miss Potter which they borrowed and hastily filled with a quantity of bundles.

'There may just have been room for the pudding,' said Samuel Whiskers wistfully.

'I notice that *you* are not pushing the barrow,' retorted Anna Maria. 'You might be of another opinion if you were!'

Then Samuel Whiskers and
Anna Maria made their way
to Farmer Potatoes' hay barn
and hauled their parcels with
a bit of string to the top of the
hay mow.

'Be quick,' urged Anna
Maria, 'and tie the bundles
on, or Miss Potter will be
missing the barrow.'

The cat family quickly recovered. The dumpling was peeled off Tom Kitten and made separately into a pudding, with currants in it to hide the smuts. They had to put Tom Kitten into a hot bath to get the butter off.

  And after that, there were no more rats for a long time at Mrs Tabitha Twitchit's.

THE
TAILOR
OF
GLOUCESTER

In the time of swords and periwigs and full-skirted coats with flowered lappets - when gentlemen wore ruffles and gold-laced waistcoats of paduasoy and taffeta - there lived a tailor in Gloucester.

He sat in the window of a little shop in Westgate Street, cross-legged on a table, from morning till night.

One bitter cold day near Christmas,
the tailor began to make a coat of
cherry-coloured corded silk.

'The finest of wedding-coats for
the Mayor of Gloucester who is to
be married on Christmas Day in the
morning,' he muttered to himself as
he worked.

The table was all littered with
cherry-coloured snippets.

'I'm sure I cannot afford to waste the smallest piece,' said the tailor as he continued cutting. 'Too narrow breadths for nought except waistcoats for mice!

'Now, the lining . . . Ah yes! Just the thing - yellow taffeta.'

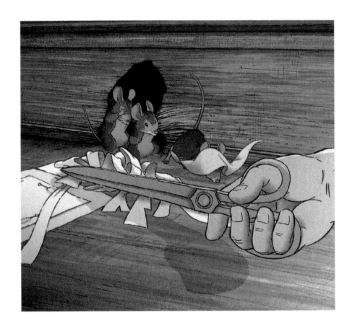

Unnoticed, little mice retrieved the scraps from his work bench and carried them off.

'By my whiskers, I cannot remember when we had silk of such quality on these premises!' exclaimed the little mouse.

'Oh, yellow taffeta - just what I would have chosen myself,' whispered another.

'My poor back,' sighed the tailor, 'but it is done. The light is fading and I am tired. All is ready to sew in the morning, except for one item - I am wanting one single skein of cherry-coloured twisted silk thread.'

The old tailor locked up his shop and shuffled home through the snow.

The mice were more fortunate and did not have to brave the cold. Using secret passages and staircases behind the wooden wainscots of all the old houses in Gloucester, they could run from house to house.

The tailor lived alone with his cat, whose name was Simpkin. All day long, while the tailor was out at work, Simpkin kept house by himself. Simpkin was also fond of the mice, but he gave them no satin for coats!

'Ah, Simpkin, old friend!' exclaimed the tailor as he arrived home. 'We shall make our fortune from this coat, but I am worn to a ravelling. Now, take this groat (which is our last fourpence) and buy a penn'orth of bread, a penn'orth of milk and a penn'orth of sausages.'

'And, Simpkin,' remembered the tailor, 'with the last penny of our fourpence buy me one penn'orth of cherry-coloured silk. But do *not* lose the last penny, Simpkin, or I am undone and worn to a thread-paper, for I have *no more twist*.'

The tailor was very tired and beginning to be ill. He sat by the hearth and talked to himself about that wonderful coat.

'The Mayor has ordered a coat and an embroidered waistcoat to be lined with yellow taffeta.'

Suddenly, interrupting him, were a number of little noises coming from the dresser at the other side of the kitchen - *Tip tap, tip tap tip!*

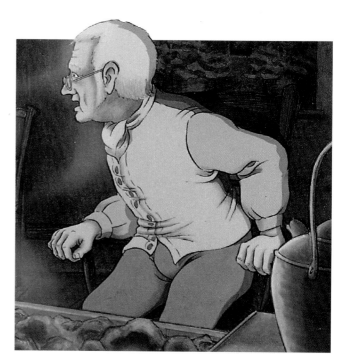

Tip tap, tip tap tip!

'Now what can that be?' the tailor wondered. He crossed the kitchen, and stood quite still beside the dresser, listening and peering through his spectacles.

Tip tap, tip tap, tip tap tip!

The tailor lifted up a teacup which was upside-down. Out stepped a little live lady mouse. Then, out from under teacups and from under bowls and basins, stepped more little mice.

'Good gracious, this is very peculiar,' remarked the tailor. 'I'll wager this is all Simpkin's doing, the rascal.

'Oh, was I wise to entrust my last fourpence to Simpkin? And was it right to let loose those mice, undoubtedly the property of Simpkin?'

Simpkin returned and opened the door with an angry 'G-r-r-miaw!' like a cat that is vexed: for he hated the snow, and there was snow in his ears, and snow in his collar at the back of his neck.

He sniffed and then looked suspiciously at the dresser - the cups and jugs had been moved! Simpkin wanted his supper of a little fat mouse.

'Simpkin,' asked the tailor anxiously, 'where is my *twist*?'

Simpkin was cross with his master,
and if he had been able to talk he would have asked:
'Where is my *mouse*?'
  He quickly hid the twist in the teapot on the dresser,
and growled at the tailor.
  'Where is my twist, Simpkin? Alack, I am undone. . . I am so weak,'
lamented the tailor and went sadly to bed.

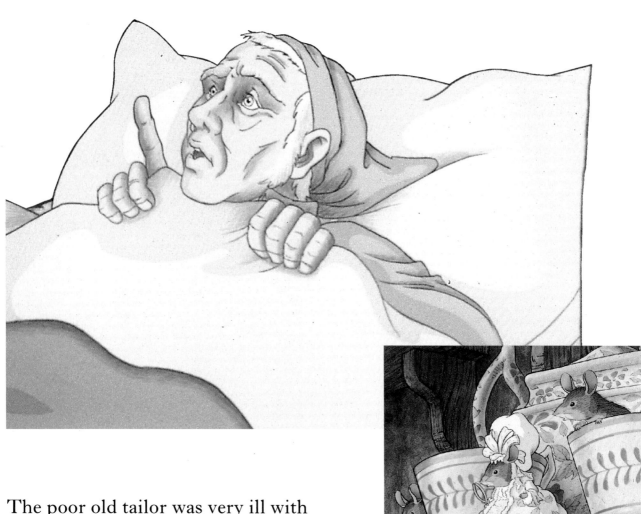

The poor old tailor was very ill with fever, tossing and turning in his four-post bed; and still in his dreams he mumbled - 'No more twist. . . one-and-twenty buttonholes. . . to be finished by noon on Saturday . . . and it is already Tuesday!'

The little mice came out again, and listened to the tailor; and they took notice of the pattern of that wonderful coat. They whispered to one another about the taffeta lining, and about little mouse tippets.

Indeed, what should become of the cherry-coloured coat?

In the tailor's shop the embroidered silk and satin lay cut out upon the table, and who should come to sew them when the window was barred and the door was fast locked?

The tailor lay ill for three days and three nights and then it was Christmas Eve and very late at night. The moon climbed up over the roofs and chimneys. All the city of Gloucester was fast asleep under the snow.

The cathedral clock struck twelve and Simpkin went out into the night.

For an old story tells how all the animals can talk in the night between Christmas Eve and Christmas Day in the morning (though very few people can hear them, or know what it is that they say).

Simpkin wandered through the streets feeling lonely and hungry.

'My master's cupboard is as empty as old Mother Hubbard's,' he complained miserably.

But when Simpkin turned a corner he saw a glow of light coming from the tailor's shop. He crept up to peep in at the window.

Inside the shop was a snippeting of scissors and a snappeting of thread and little mouse voices were singing loudly and happily:
'Three little mice sat down to spin,
Pussy passed by and she peeped in.'

Simpkin miaowed to get in but the door was locked.

'Dear me, and the key is under the tailor's pillow,' mocked a little mouse seamstress gleefully.

Simpkin came away from the shop and went home. There he found the poor old tailor without fever, sleeping peacefully.

121

Then Simpkin went on tip-toe and took a little parcel of silk out of the teapot - he felt quite ashamed of his badness compared with those good little mice!

When the tailor awoke the next morning, the first thing which he saw upon the patchwork quilt, was a skein of cherry-coloured twisted silk, and beside it the repentant Simpkin!

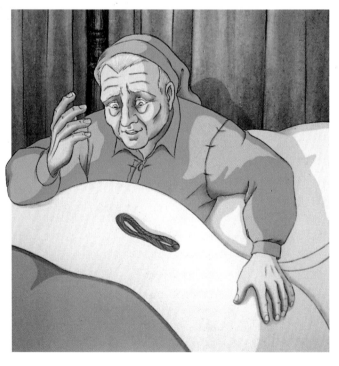

The tailor got up and dressed and went out into the street.

'I have my twist,' he said to himself, 'but no more strength nor time than will serve to make me one single buttonhole; for this is Christmas Day in the morning! The Mayor of Gloucester is to be married by noon - and where is his cherry-coloured coat?'

He unlocked the door of the little shop and looked in amazement.

There, where he had left plain
cuttings of silk now lay the most
beautiful coat and embroidered satin
waistcoat that ever were worn by a
Mayor of Gloucester!

Everything was finished except for
one single cherry-coloured
buttonhole, and where that
buttonhole was wanting there was
pinned a scrap of paper with these
words - in little teeny weeny
writing - NO MORE TWIST.

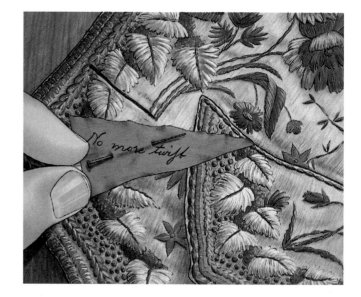

And from then began the luck of the Tailor of Gloucester; he grew quite stout, and he grew quite rich.

Never were seen such ruffles, or such embroidered cuffs. But his buttonholes were the greatest triumph - the stitches were *so* neat and *so* small they looked as if they had been made by little mice!

THE TALE OF THE FLOPSY BUNNIES AND MRS TITTLEMOUSE

It is said that the effect of eating too much lettuce is "soporific."
I have never felt sleepy after eating lettuces; but then I am not a rabbit.
They certainly had a very soporific effect upon the Flopsy Bunnies!
  When Benjamin Bunny grew up, he married his Cousin Flopsy.
They had a large family, and they were very improvident and cheerful.
I do not remember the separate names of their children; they were
generally called the "Flopsy Bunnies".

As there was not always quite enough to eat, Benjamin used to borrow cabbages from Flopsy's brother, Peter Rabbit, who kept a nursery garden.

Sometimes Peter Rabbit had no cabbages to spare. When this happened, the Flopsy Bunnies went across the field to a rubbish heap, in the ditch outside Mr McGregor's garden.

Mr McGregor's rubbish heap was a mixture. There were jam pots and paper bags, and some rotten vegetable marrows and an old boot or two. One day – oh joy! – there were a quantity of overgrown lettuces.

A little wood-mouse was picking over the rubbish among the jam pots. Her name was Mrs Tittlemouse.

"Good afternoon, Ma'am," said Benjamin Bunny. "Pray excuse my youngsters – they have waited overlong for their lunch today!"

"Then I think I shall go home," said Mrs Tittlemouse, "before I am eaten in mistake for a lettuce!"

Mrs Tittlemouse lived alone
in a bank under a hedge.
Such a funny house!

There were yards and yards
of sandy passages, leading to
storerooms and nut and seed
cellars.

There was a kitchen, a parlour,
a pantry, and a larder. Also,
there was Mrs Tittlemouse's
bedroom, where she slept in a
little box bed!

Mrs Tittlemouse was a most
terribly particular little mouse,
always sweeping and dusting
the soft sandy floors.

Sometimes a beetle lost its way
in the passages. "Shuh! shuh!
little dirty feet!" said Mrs
Tittlemouse, clattering her
dust-pan.

And one day a little old woman
ran up and down in a red spotty
cloak. "Your house is on fire,
Mother Ladybird! Fly away
home to your children!"

Another day, a big fat spider
came in to shelter from the rain.
"Beg pardon, is this not Miss
Muffet's?" "Go away, you bold
bad spider! Leaving ends of
cobweb all over my nice clean
house!" Mrs Tittlemouse
bundled the spider out at a
window.

It was dinner time. "I shall go to my furthest storeroom and fetch cherry stones and thistle-down seed..." said Mrs Tittlemouse. Suddenly round a corner, she met Babbitty Bumble. "Zizz, Bizz, Bizz!" said the bumble bee, in a peevish squeak, and she sidled down a side passage.

Three or four other bees buzzed fiercely. "I am not in the habit of letting lodgings; this is an intrusion!" said Mrs Tittlemouse crossly. "I will have them turned out! I wonder who would help me? . . . Mr Benjamin Bunny, of course! Benjamin Bunny will help me drive out these tiresome bees!"

Mrs Tittlemouse went back to the rubbish heap.

The Flopsy Bunnies had simply stuffed lettuces and by degrees, one after another, they had been overcome with slumber.

Benjamin was not so much overcome as his children. Before going to sleep he was sufficiently wide awake to put a paper bag over his head to keep off the flies. The little Flopsy Bunnies slept delightfully in the warm sun.

Mrs Tittle-mouse rustled across the paper bag, and awakened Benjamin Bunny.

"Mr Benjamin, I am so sorry to disturb you, but as we are both acquainted with Mr Peter Rabbit I thought to ask a favour of you... oh Mr Benjamin, I am having such trouble with *bees* in my house!"

"Bees, yes, indeed Ma'am, very tiresome creatures," said Benjamin sleepily.

A robin arrived with a whir of wings and a flash of red. "Oh, Mr Red-breast!" said Mrs Tittlemouse, "could *you* help me with my nest of bees?"

Then they heard a heavy tread above their heads. Mr McGregor was approaching. "The Flopsy Bunnies! Mr McGregor is sure to see the Flopsy Bunnies," said Mrs Tittlemouse. "We must wake them up, we must warn them!" But it was impossible to wake the Flopsy Bunnies.

The robin darted around Mr McGregor's head, trying to distract him. Suddenly, he emptied out a sackful of lawn mowings right upon the top of the sleeping Flopsy Bunnies! Benjamin shrank down under his paper bag. Mrs Tittlemouse hid in a jam pot.

The little rabbits smiled sweetly in their sleep under the shower of grass. Mr McGregor looked down. He saw some funny little brown tips of ears sticking up through the lawn mowings. He stared at them for some time.

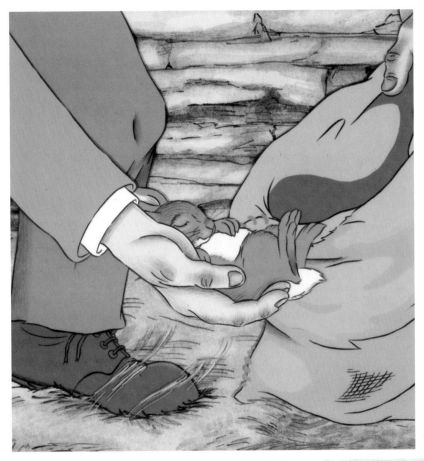

Presently a fly settled on one of them and it moved. Mr McGregor climbed down on to the rubbish heap – "One, two, three, four! five! six leetle rabbits!" said he as he dropped them into his sack.

Mr McGregor tied up the sack and left it on the wall. He went to put away the mowing machine.

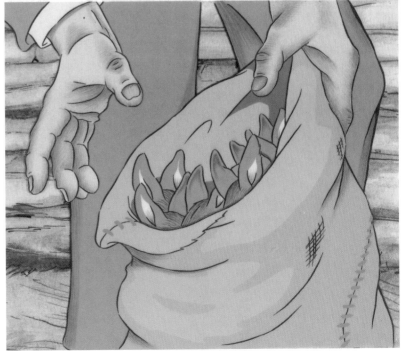

Then Mrs Tittlemouse came out of her jam pot, and Benjamin took the
paper bag off his head. They could see the sack, up on the wall.
Just then Mrs Flopsy Bunny (who had remained at home) came across
the field.

She looked suspiciously at the sack and wondered where everybody was?
"Mr McGregor has caught your babies and put them in this sack!" said
Mrs Tittlemouse.

Benjamin and Flopsy were in despair; they could not undo the string.

"My poor babies, what shall we do?" said Flopsy. But Mrs Tittlemouse was a resourceful person. "Why, Mrs Tittlemouse, whatever can you be doing?" said Benjamin. She was nibbling a hole in the bottom corner of the sack!

The little rabbits were pulled out and pinched to wake them.

Their parents stuffed the empty
sack with three rotten vegetable
marrows, an old blacking-
brush and two decayed
turnips.

"We'll see what old
McGregor thinks about
that!" said Benjamin, and
they all hid under a bush
and watched for him.

Mrs Tittlemouse hastily
said goodday and went home.

Mr McGregor had come back to fetch the sack. He carried it off carefully, for he believed the Flopsy Bunnies were still sleeping peacefully inside, but if he had looked behind he would have seen them following at a safe distance!

They watched him go into his house, and then they crept up to the window to listen.

Mr McGregor threw down the sack on the stone floor. "One, two, three, four, five, six leetle rabbits!" said Mr McGregor.
(The youngest Flopsy Bunny got upon the window-sill.)

Mrs McGregor took hold of the sack and felt it. She untied the sack and put her hand inside. When she felt the vegetables she became very very angry.

A rotten marrow came flying through the kitchen window, and hit the youngest Flopsy Bunny. It was rather hurt.

Then Benjamin and Flopsy thought it was time to go home.

What a surprise awaited Mrs Tittlemouse on her return home! When she got back to the parlour, she heard some one coughing in a fat voice, and there sat Mr Jackson! "How do you do, Mr Jackson? Deary me, you have got very wet feet!" said Mrs Tittlemouse. "Thank you, thank you, thank you, Mrs Tittlemouse! I'll sit awhile and dry myself," said Mr Jackson. He sat and smiled, and the water dripped off his coat tails. Mrs Tittlemouse went round with a mop.

He sat such a while that he had to be asked if he would take some dinner? First she offered him some cherry stones. "No teeth, no teeth, no teeth!" mumbled Mr Jackson, opening his mouth unnecessarily wide; he certainly had not a tooth in his head.

"Thistledown seed, Mr Jackson?" "Tiddly, widdly, widdly! Pouff, pouff, puff!" said Mr Jackson. He blew the thistledown all over the room.

"Thank you, thank you, thank you, Mrs Tittlemouse, but what I really – *really* should like – would be a dish of honey! I can smell it, that's why I came to call." He rose ponderously from the table, and began to look into the cupboards. Mrs Tittlemouse followed with a dish-cloth.

Mr Jackson began to walk down the passage. "Indeed, indeed, you will stick fast, Mr Jackson!" said Mrs Tittlemouse. They went along the sandy passage – "Tiddly widdly –"

"Buzz! Wizz! Wizz!" He met Babbitty round a corner, and snapped her up, and put her down again. "I do not like bumble bees, they are all over bristles," said Mr Jackson, wiping his mouth with his coat sleeve.

"Get out, you nasty old toad!" shrieked Babbitty Bumble. "I shall go distracted!" scolded Mrs Tittlemouse.

146

Mr Jackson pulled out the bees nest and ate the honey. He seemed to
have no objection to stings. The bees gathered up their pollen-bags and
flew away, down the passages and out of the windows and doors of the
little house, and away over the fields, to find a quieter place for their
nest. Mrs Tittlemouse shut herself in the nut cellar.

When Mrs Tittlemouse ventured out of the nut cellar, everybody had gone away. But the untidiness was something dreadful. She went out and fetched some twigs, to partly close up the front door. "I will make it too small for Mr Jackson!"

But she was too tired to do any more. First she fell asleep in her chair, and then she went to bed. "Will it ever be tidy again?" said poor Mrs Tittlemouse.

Next morning she got up very early and did a spring cleaning which lasted a fortnight.

When it was all beautifully neat and clean, she gave a party to five other mice, without Mr Jackson. He smelt the party and came up the bank, but he could not squeeze in at the door. Mrs Tittlemouse had quite forgiven him, and although she had no food to suit his taste, she handed him out acorn-cupfuls of honey-dew through the window, and he was not at all offended.

The flopsy Bunnies did not forget Mrs Tittlemouse.
Next Christmas Thomasina Tittlemouse got a present of
enough rabbit-wool to make herself a cloak and a hood,
and a handsome muff and a pair of warm mittens.

THE END

THE TALE OF
Mrs Tiggy-Winkle
AND
Mr Jeremy Fisher

Once upon a time there was a little girl called Lucie, who lived at a farm
called Little-town. She was a good little girl — only she was *always*
losing her handkerchiefs! "That's three handkins and a pinafore. Oh dear!
Have you seen them, Tabby Kitten?"

The kitten went on washing her white paws; so Lucie asked a speckled hen — "Sally Henny-Penny, have *you* found three pocket-handkins?"

But the speckled hen ran away, clucking.

Then Lucie asked Cock Robin. He looked sideways at Lucie with his bright black eye, and flew over a stile and away.

Lucie scrambled up the hill behind Little-town as fast as her stout legs would carry her. "Excuse me sir," Lucie asked Mr Jeremy Fisher, "have you seen my pocket-handkins or even a pinafore?"

"I'm afraid not, young lady," he replied.

Then Lucie saw some pieces of white on the hillside. "They might just be my pocket-handkins," she said.

Presently Lucie came to a spring, bubbling out from the hillside. "Goodness! Who could have put such a tiny bucket there — it's no bigger than an egg-cup! And look at those little foot marks," remarked Lucie. She followed the footprints until she reached a little door in the hillside.

Lucie knocked - once - twice, and a little frightened voice called out "Oh! Who's that?"

"I'm Lucie. I didn't mean to startle you, but who are you? And have you seen my pocket handkins?"

"Oh, yes, if you please'm. My name
is Mrs Tiggy-winkle. Please do
make yourself comfortable," said
the little person and she started to
iron something.

"What's that?" asked Lucie.
"That's not my pocket handkin."

"Oh no," Mrs Tiggy-winkle
replied, "that's a little scarlet
waistcoat belonging to Cock Robin."

"And, if you please'm, that's a damask tablecloth belonging to Jenny Wren."

"There's one of my pocket handkins," said Lucie, searching through the clothes-basket, "and look, there's my pinny!"

"Fancy that," said Mrs Tiggy-winkle, "they were there all the time. I'll just put the iron over them."

"There!" exclaimed Mrs Tiggy-winkle proudly, holding up Lucie's newly ironed pinny.

"Oh, that *is* lovely!" said Lucie gratefully.

"Goodness, what are they?" asked Lucie pointing to some long yellow things.

"That's a pair of stockings belonging to Sally Henny-penny."

"There's another handkersniff, but it's red," said Lucie.

"That one belongs to Mrs Rabbit and it did so smell of onions, I've had to wash it separately."

"And these are woolly coats belonging to the little lambs at Skelghyl. Now then, I always have to starch these little dicky shirt-fronts. They're Tom Titmouse's and he's most terrible particular."

"I'll just hang these up to air. I'd take it very kindly'm if you would hand the things up to me."

Lucie held up a tattered blue jacket.

"Now there's a story," said Mrs Tiggy-winkle. "Young master Peter Rabbit had a narrow escape from Mr McGregor's garden, but his jacket was left behind, and what with the rain and all . . ."

With all the washing hung up to dry, Mrs Tiggy-winkle and Lucie sat down to take some tea.

Then they tied up all the clothes in bundles and set off to deliver the clean washing.

All the little animals and birds were very much obliged to dear Mrs Tiggy-winkle, and when they came to the bottom of the hill there was nothing left to carry except one little bundle that belonged to Mr Jeremy Fisher.

"I do believe I saw him fishing when I was searching for my handkins," said Lucie as they approached the little house by the pond.

"Ladies, ahoy," greeted Mr Jeremy Fisher.

"I was just about to leave your clean washing and collect from the porch as usual," said Mrs Tiggy-winkle.

"Ah yes, I mean, no, dear lady," said Mr Jeremy, as Mrs Tiggy-winkle held up his torn mackintosh. "Little mishap . . . er, more of an accident . . . very nearly fatal. Skin of my teeth and all that!

"A really frightful thing it would have been, had I not been wearing my mackintosh — but let me start from the beginning . . ." and Mr Jeremy began to tell his story.

The day had started so well for Mr Jeremy Fisher.

"Ah! Nice drop of rain, be good fishing today I shouldn't wonder. I will get some worms and catch a dish of minnows for my dinner. If I catch more than five fish, I will invite my friends Mr Alderman Ptolemy Tortoise and Sir Isaac Newton."

"Now then, my mackintosh, and goloshes. Mmm . . . where did I leave my sandwiches?"

Mr Jeremy Fisher set off with
hops to the place where he kept his
boat.

"I know just the place for minnows,"
he said and pushed the boat into
open water.

He settled himself cross-legged and
arranged his fishing tackle.

The rain trickled down his back and for nearly an hour he stared at
the float. "This is getting tiresome. I foresee, I fear, an adjustment to the
dinner menu. I will eat a butterfly sandwich and wait till the shower is
over."

But then a great water-beetle came up underneath the lily leaf and tweaked the toe of one of Mr Jeremy's galoshes. "You beastly creature," he complained. Then he heard a splash from the bank. "I trust that is not a rat," he said crossly. "Is there no peace to be had anywhere?" and he punted off to find a quieter spot.

Then a little girl asked him if he'd seen her lost handkins.

"I'm afraid not, young lady," he replied. "Dear me, whatever would I be doing with pocket handkins and pinafores, indeed," he chuckled.

But then there was a bobbing of the float and a tugging of the line. "A minnow! A minnow! I have him by the nose! Hooray!"

But Mr Jeremy Fisher got a horrible surprise. He had landed little Jack Sharp, the stickleback.

"Ouch! Jack Sharp – what are you doing on the end of my line? Get off my boat this instant!"

Mr Jeremy sat disconsolately on the edge of his boat worrying about what he would give his guests for dinner.

Then suddenly a *much* worse thing happened. A great big enormous trout came up — ker-pflop-p-p-p! — and seized Mr Jeremy with a snap.

Then it turned and dived down to the bottom of the pond!

But luckily the trout did not like the taste of Mr Jeremy Fisher's mackintosh and spat him out again. He scrambled out on to the nearest bank.

"Never, *never*, have I been so glad to see the light of day," he gasped. "What a mercy it was not a pike! Just look at my best mackintosh — all in tatters."

" . . . And that is what happened," finished Mr Jeremy Fisher. "It was a nightmare, I assure you, truly frightful."

"Oh, mercy me!" exclaimed Mrs Tiggy-winkle anxiously.

"Oh, Miss Lucie," said
Mrs Tiggy-winkle, "here are
Mr Jeremy Fisher's guests. We
must be on our way. I will do
my best with your things sir."

Mr Jeremy and his friends sat down
to dinner. "Perhaps we might take a
glass of pond wine with our roast
grasshopper and ladybird sauce?"

And Mrs Tiggy-winkle hurried home not stopping to give Lucie a bill
for the washing.

Lucie watched her as she went and wondered, "But where is your cap
and your shawl and your gown? If I didn't know better,
Mrs Tiggy-winkle, I would think that you were nothing but a *hedgehog*!"

THE TALE OF
MR TOD

*A story about two disagreeable people
called Tommy Brock and Mr Tod*

Old Mr Bouncer sat in the spring sunshine outside the burrow, in a muffler, smoking a pipe of rabbit tobacco.

Old Mr Bouncer was stricken in years. He lived with his son Benjamin Bunny and his daughter-in-law Flopsy, who had a young family.

"Now take care of the children Uncle Bouncer," said Flopsy, "we're going out visiting for a while."

The little rabbit-babies were just old enough to open their blue eyes and kick. They lay in a fluffy bed of rabbit wool and hay, in a shallow burrow, separate from the main rabbit hole. To tell the truth – old Mr Bouncer had forgotten them.

Tommy Brock was passing through the woods, with a sack and a little spade which he used for digging, and some mole traps. He was looking for food. Tommy Brock was friendly with old Mr Bouncer; they agreed in disliking Mr Tod.

Old Mr Bouncer sat in the sun, and conversed cordially with Tommy Brock. "What's the news from down hill, Tommy my dear fellow?" said Mr Bouncer. "Not so good I'm sorry to say," said Tommy Brock, "I have not had a good square meal in a fortnight. I shall have to turn vegetarian and eat my own tail!" It was not much of a joke, but old Mr Bouncer laughed. "My dear old chap, won't you step inside for a slice of seed cake and a glass of homemade cowslip wine to fortify the constitution," he said.

Tommy Brock squeezed himself into the rabbit hole with alacrity. "Have a cabbage leaf cigar, Tommy, go on," said old Mr Bouncer, who was smoking his pipe. Smoke filled the burrow. Old Mr Bouncer coughed and laughed; and Tommy Brock puffed and grinned.

Mr Bouncer laughed and coughed. "I don't get many visitors, not like it used to be," he mumbled sleepily. He slumped lower in his chair and shut his eyes because of the cabbage smoke . . .

Tommy Brock waited a few moments to be sure that old Mr Bouncer was fast asleep. Then he put all the young rabbit-babies into his sack.

When Flopsy and Benjamin came back – old Mr Bouncer woke up. "Uncle Bouncer, where are the children?" said Flopsy, anxiously. "Father, where are the babies?" asked Benjamin. But Mr Bouncer would not confess that he had admitted anybody into the rabbit hole.

The smell of badger was
undeniable, and there were
round heavy footmarks in
the sand. Mr Bouncer was in
disgrace; Flopsy wrung her
ears, and slapped him. "It's
old Tommy Brock, he's
taken our babies," she cried.
"Now don't worry,
Flopsy," said Benjamin,
"I'll catch that old rogue."
Benjamin Bunny set
off at once after
Tommy
Brock.

There was not much difficulty in tracking him;
Benjamin soon found his footmarks. He had gone
slowly up the winding footpath through the

wood, and his heavy
steps showed plainly in
the mud.

The path led to a part of the thicket where the trees had been cleared; there were leafy oak stumps, and a sea of blue hyacinths – but the smell that made Benjamin stop, was *not* the smell of flowers!

Mr Tod's stick house was before him and, for once,

Mr Tod was at home. Inside the stick house somebody dropped a plate, and said something. Benjamin stamped his foot, and bolted.

He never stopped until he came to the other side of the wood.

Apparently Tommy Brock had turned the same way. Upon the top of the wall, some ravellings of a sack had caught on a bramble bush.

185

It was getting late in the afternoon. Other rabbits were coming out to enjoy the evening air. "Cousin Peter! Peter Rabbit, Peter Rabbit!" shouted Benjamin Bunny. "Whatever is the matter, Cousin Benjamin?" asked Peter. "He's bagged my family – Tommy Brock – in a sack, have you seen him?"

Peter had seen Tommy Brock, carrying a sack with "something live in it".

"Cousin Benjamin, compose yourself," he said. "Tommy Brock has gone to Mr Tod's other house at the top of Bull Banks."

And Peter accompanied the afflicted parent, who was all of a twitter. "Hurry Peter; he will be cooking them; come quicker!" said Benjamin Bunny.

Tommy Brock was already in Mr Tod's kitchen, making preparations for supper. (Mr Tod had half a dozen houses, but he was seldom at home. The houses were not always empty when Mr Tod moved *out*; because sometimes Tommy Brock moved *in,* without asking leave).

The sunshine was still warm and slanting on the hill pastures. Half way up, Cotton-tail was sitting in her doorway, with four or five half-grown little rabbits playing about her; one black and the others brown. She had

seen Tommy Brock passing. He had rested nearby a while, pointed to the sack, and seemed doubled up with laughing.

"Squirrel Nutkin, have you seen Tommy Brock?" asked Peter. But he hadn't.

In the wood at Bull Banks, the trees grew amongst heaped up rocks; and there, beneath a crag – Mr Tod had made one of his homes.

The rabbits crept up carefully, listening and peeping. The setting sun made the window panels glow like red flame; but the kitchen fire was not alight. Benjamin sighed with relief. No person was to be seen, and no young rabbits. But the preparations for one person's supper on the table made him shudder.

Then they scrambled round to the other side of the house, and crept up to the bedroom window. As their eyes became accustomed to the darkness, they perceived that somebody was asleep, lying under a blanket. Tommy Brock's snores came, grunty and regular, from Mr Tod's bed.

They went back to the front of the house, and tried in every way to move the bolt of the kitchen window. They tried to push up a rusty nail between the window sashes; but it was of no use, especially without a light.

In half an hour the moon rose over the wood, and shone full and clear and cold, in at the kitchen window. The light showed a little door beside the kitchen fireplace, belonging to a brick oven. Presently Peter and Benjamin noticed that whenever they shook the window, the little door opposite shook in answer. The young family were alive, shut up in the oven!

They sat side by side outside the window, whispering. There was really not very much comfort in the discovery. Although the young family was alive, the little rabbits were quite incapable of letting themselves out; they were not old enough to crawl.

After much debate, Peter and Benjamin

decided to dig a tunnel. "It's the only way. A tunnel right under the house, and into the kitchen." They began to burrow a yard or two lower down the bank. They dug and dug for hours and hours. They could not tunnel straight on account of stones; but by the end of the night they were under the kitchen floor. It was morning – sunrise.

From the fields down below there came the angry cry of a jay – followed by the sharp yelping bark of a fox! Then those two rabbits lost their heads completely. They did the most foolish thing that they could have done. They rushed into their short new tunnel, and hid themselves at the top end of it, under Mr Tod's kitchen floor.

Mr Tod was coming up Bull Banks, and he was in the very worst of tempers. "Badger . . . Badger . . . I can smell Badger," he fumed, and slapped his stick upon the earth; he guessed where Tommy Brock had gone to.

Mr Tod approached his house very carefully with a large rusty key, and went in. The sight of the table all set out for supper made him furious. But what absorbed Mr Tod's attention was a noise – a deep slow regular snoring grunting noise, coming from his own bed. He peeped around the half-open bedroom door.

Mr Tod came out of the house in a hurry; he scratched up the earth with fury. His whiskers bristled and his coat-collar stood on end with rage. "Badger . . . Badger . . . in my house, in my bed, I'll fix that Badger." He fetched a clothes line and went back into the bedroom.

He stood a minute watching Tommy Brock and listening to the loud snores. Then Mr Tod turned his back towards the bed and undid the window. It creaked; he turned round with a jump. Tommy Brock, who had opened one eye – shut it hastily. The snores continued. Mr Tod pushed the greater part of the clothes line out of the window.

Mr Tod went out at the front door, and round to the back of the house. He took up the coil of line from the window sill, listened for a moment, (Tommy Brock snored conscientiously), and then tied the rope to a tree. "I will wake him with an unpleasant surprise," he said.

Mr Tod fetched a large heavy pailful of water from the spring, and staggered with it through the kitchen into his bedroom. Tommy Brock snored industriously, with rather a snort. He was lying on his back with his mouth open, grinning from ear to ear. One eye was still not perfectly shut.

Then Mr Tod put down the pail, and took up the end of the rope with a hook attached. He gingerly mounted a chair by the head of the bedstead. His legs were dangerously near to Tommy Brock's teeth. He reached up and put the end of rope over the head of the bed, where the curtains ought to hang.

Mr Tod, who was a thin-legged person (though vindictive and sandy whiskered) – was quite unable to lift the heavy weight of the full pail of water to the level of the hook and rope. After much thought he emptied the water into a wash-basin and jug.

The empty pail was not too heavy for him; he slung it up wobbling over the head of Tommy Brock. Surely there never was such a sleeper! Mr Tod got up and down, down and up on the chair.

As he could not lift the whole pailful of water at once, he fetched a milk jug, and ladled quarts of water into the pail by degrees. The pail got fuller and fuller, and swung like a pendulum. Occasionally a drop splashed over; but still Tommy Brock snored regularly and never moved – except one eye.

At last Mr Tod's preparations were complete. "It will make a great mess in my bedroom; but I could never sleep in that bed again without a spring cleaning of some sort," said Mr Tod, and softly left the room. He ran round behind the house, to the tree. He was obliged to gnaw the rope with his teeth – he chewed and gnawed for more then twenty minutes.

The moment he had gone, Tommy Brock got up in a hurry. He peered out of the window and saw Mr Tod

gnawing on the rope.

Tommy Brock rolled Mr Tod's dressing-gown into a bundle, put it into the bed beneath the pail of water instead of himself, and left the room also – grinning immensely. He went into the kitchen, lighted the fire and boiled the kettle; for the moment he did not trouble himself to cook the baby rabbits.

At last the rope snapped. Inside the house there was a great crash and splash.

But no screams. Mr Tod listened attentively. Then he peeped in at the window. In the middle of the bed under the blanket, was a wet flattened *something* – its head was covered by the wet blanket and it was *not snoring any longer*. Mr Tod's eyes glistened. "This has turned out even better than I expected," said Mr Tod. "I will bury that nasty person in a hole. I will have a thorough disinfecting with soap to remove the smell." He hurried round the house to get a shovel . . .

. . . He opened the door . . . Tommy Brock was sitting at Mr Tod's kitchen table, pouring tea from Mr Tod's tea-pot into Mr Tod's tea-cup. He was quite dry, and he was grinning. He threw a cup of scalding tea all over Mr Tod.

Then Mr Tod rushed upon Tommy Brock, and Tommy Brock grappled with Mr Tod amongst the broken crockery, and there was a terrific battle all over the kitchen. To the rabbits underneath, it sounded as if the floor would give way at each crash of falling furniture.

Inside the house the racket was fearful. The rabbit babies in the oven woke up trembling; perhaps it was fortunate they were shut up inside. Everything was broken; the crockery was smashed to atoms. Tommy Brock put his foot in a jar of raspberry jam.

The kettle fell off the hob, and the boiling water out of the kettle fell upon the tail of Mr Tod. Tommy Brock rolled Mr Tod over and over like a log, out at the door.

"Let's get out of here, Benjamin," said Peter. The two rabbits crept out of their tunnel, and hung about amongst the rocks and bushes, listening anxiously.

Tommy Brock and Mr Tod rolled over and over. The snarling and worrying went on, and they rolled over the bank, and down hill, bumping over the rocks. There would never be any love lost between Tommy Brock and Mr Tod.

As soon as the coast was clear, Peter Rabbit and Benjamin Bunny came out of the bushes – "Run for it! Run in, Cousin Benjamin! Run in and get them! While I watch the door."

In Mr Tod's kitchen, amongst the wreckage, Benjamin Bunny picked his way to the oven nervously, through a thick cloud of dust. He opened the oven door, felt inside, and found something warm and

wriggling. He lifted it out carefully, and rejoined Peter Rabbit outside.

At home in the rabbit hole, things had not been quite comfortable.

After quarrelling at supper, Flopsy and old Mr Bouncer had passed a sleepless night, and quarrelled again at breakfast.

Old Mr Bouncer could no longer deny that he had invited company into the rabbit

hole, but he refused to reply to the questions and reproaches of Flopsy. The day passed heavily.

The two breathless
rabbits came scuttering
away down Bull Banks,
Benjamin half carrying,
half dragging a sack,
bumpetty bump over
the grass. They reached
home safely and burst
into the rabbit hole.

Great was old Mr
Bouncer's relief and
Flopsy's joy when
Peter and
Benjamin arrived
in triumph with
the young family.
"Benjamin, Peter – oh,
thank goodness you're all safe," said Flopsy.
"I was a bit worried myself, actually," admitted Mr Bouncer.

Old Mr Bouncer was forgiven. The rabbit-babies were rather tumbled and very hungry; they were fed and put to bed. They soon recovered. Then Peter and Benjamin told their story – but they had not waited long enough to be able to tell the end of the battle between Tommy Brock and Mr Tod.

THE END

THE TALE OF
TWO BAD MICE
AND
JOHNNY TOWN-MOUSE

Once upon a time there was a very beautiful doll's-house; it was red brick with white windows, and it had a front door and a chimney.

It belonged to two dolls called Lucinda and Jane. Jane was the cook; but she never did any cooking, because the dinner had been bought ready-made, in a box full of shavings.

One morning Lucinda and Jane went out for a drive in the doll's perambulator. There was no one in the nursery and it was very quiet.

Presently, there was a little scratching noise in the corner where there was a mouse-hole under the skirting-board. Tom Thumb put out his head. A minute afterwards, Hunca Munca, his wife, put her head out too.

When they saw that there was no one in the nursery, they went cautiously across the hearthrug.

Hunca Munca pushed the front door — it was not locked. "Let's have a look inside" she said.

Tom Thumb and Hunca Munca went upstairs and peeped into the dining-room. Such a lovely dinner was laid out upon the table! There were tin spoons, and lead knives and forks, and two dolly-chairs. "All ready for us!" said Tom Thumb.

Tom Thumb set to work at once to carve the ham, but the knife crumpled up and hurt him; he put his finger in his mouth. "It's not cooked enough. It's hard. You have a try Hunca Munca."

Hunca Munca stood up in her chair, and chopped at the ham with another lead knife. The ham broke off the plate with a jerk, and rolled under the table.

"Let it alone," said Tom Thumb; "give me some fish, Hunca Munca!"

Hunca Munca tried every tin spoon in turn; the fish was glued to the dish.

Then Tom Thumb lost his temper. He put the ham in the middle of the floor, and hit it with the tongs and with the shovel — bang, bang, smash, smash! The ham flew all into pieces. Underneath the shiny paint it was made of nothing but plaster!

"It's no good. You can't eat it!" said Hunca Munca.

Then there was no end to the rage and disappointment of Tom Thumb and Hunca Munca. They broke up the pudding, the lobsters, the pears and the oranges. As the fish would not come off the plate, they put it into the red-hot crinkly paper fire in the kitchen; but it would not burn either.

Tom Thumb went up the chimney and looked out at the top — there was no soot. Hunca Munca found some tiny cans upon the dresser, labelled Rice, Coffee, Sago, but there was nothing inside except red and blue beads.

Then the mice went into the dolls' bedroom. Tom threw Jane's clothes out of the window. Hunca Munca bounced on the bed. After pulling half the feathers out of Lucinda's bolster, she remembered that she herself needed a feather bed. "Let's take this bolster back to our place," she said.

They carried the bolster downstairs and across the hearthrug. "I hope this will be worth all this work," said Tom Thumb. It was difficult to squeeze the bolster into the mouse-hole, but they managed it somehow.

"There. That's lovely!" said Hunca Munca. "Now let's go back and see what else will be useful."

They went back and fetched a chair, a book-case, a bird-cage, and several small odds and ends. The book-case and the bird-cage would not go into the mouse-hole. Hunca Munca left them behind the coal-box, and went to fetch a cradle. "This will be fine for my babies," she said.

Hunca Munca was just returning with another chair, when suddenly there was a noise of talking outside upon the landing. The mice rushed back to their hole, and the dolls came into the nursery.

What a sight met the eyes of Jane and Lucinda!

"What has happened?" asked the little girl who owned the dolls-house.

"It must be mice!" said the nurse.

The book-case and the bird-cage were rescued from under the coal-box — but Hunca Munca has got the cradle, and some of Lucinda's clothes.

She also has some useful pots and pans, and several other things.

The little girl said, "I will get a policeman doll!"

But the nurse said, "I will set a mouse-trap!"

Hunca Munca and Tom Thumb were not the only mice causing trouble that day.

When the cook opened the vegetable hamper, out sprang a terrified Timmy Willie.

"A mouse! A mouse! Call the cat!" screamed the cook.

But Timmy Willie did not wait for the cat. He rushed along the skirting-board till he came to a little hole, and in he popped.

He dropped half a foot, and crashed into the middle of a mouse dinner-party, breaking three glasses.

"Who in the world is this?" inquired Johnny Town-mouse. But after the first exclamation of surprise, he instantly recovered his manners.

He introduced Timmy to nine other mice, all with long tails and white neck-ties. The dinner was of eight courses; not much of anything, but truly elegant. Timmy was very anxious to behave with good manners, but the continual noise upstairs made him so nervous that he dropped a plate.

"Never mind, they don't belong to us," said Johnny. "How did you come here?" he asked.

"I'm from the country," said Timmy Willie. He explained how he had seen the hamper by the garden gate and climbed in. After eating some peas, he had fallen fast asleep. He awoke in a fright, while the vegetable hamper was lifted into the carrier's cart.

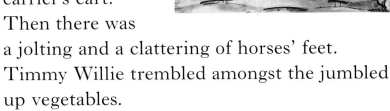

Then there was a jolting and a clattering of horses' feet. Timmy Willie trembled amongst the jumbled up vegetables.

At last the cart stopped at a house and the hamper was carried in and set down.

The cook lifted the hamper lid and screamed at the sight of poor Timmy Willie.

"Then I fell in here," finished Timmy.

"And you are most welcome," said Johnny Town-mouse.

217

Timmy Willie felt quite faint. "Would you like to go to bed?" said Johnny. "I will show you a most comfortable sofa pillow".

"It is the best bed and I keep it exclusively for visitors," said Johnny Town-mouse. But the sofa smelt of cat. Timmy Willie preferred to spend a miserable night under the fender.

  "Oh dear, oh dear!" he sighed. "I wish I was home."

The next day things were no better for Timmy Willie. He could not eat the food, and the noise prevented him from sleeping. In a few days he grew so thin that Johnny Town-mouse questioned him. "Are you ill?"

"Oh no," replied Timmy, "but I do so miss my peaceful sunny bank and my friend, Cock Robin."

"Well," said Johnny Town-mouse, "it may be that your teeth and digestion are unaccustomed to our food. Perhaps it might be wiser for you to return the way you came — in the hamper, to your own home in the country."

"Oh? Oh!" cried Timmy.

"Why of course. Did you not know that the hamper goes back empty on Saturdays?" said Johnny, rather huffily.

So Timmy Willie said goodbye to his new friends and hid in the hamper with a crumb of cake.

After much jolting, he was set down safely in his own garden.

"How good to be back!" said Timmy, in delight.

Sometimes on Saturdays he went to look at the hamper lying by the gate, but he knew better than to get in again. And nobody got out, though Johnny Town-mouse had half promised a visit.

*

Timmy Willie slept through the winter and the sun came out again in Spring.

Timmy Willie had nearly forgotten his visit to
the town, when up the sandy path all spick
and span with a brown leather bag came
Johnny Town-mouse!

Timmy Willie received him with open arms.
"You have come at the best of times. We will
have herb pudding and sit in the sun."

"Hmm! It is a little damp" said Johnny
Town-mouse.

"How are Tom Thumb and all our friends?" asked Timmy.

Johnny explained that the family had gone to the seaside. The cook was doing spring cleaning, with particular instructions to clear out the mice. There were four kittens and the cat had killed the canary.

"Tom Thumb has told the small mice all about the trap, and Hunca Munca has become quite good friends with the policeman-doll, although he never says anything, and always looks quite stern," said Johnny.

"What is that fearful noise?" asked Johnny Town-mouse.

"Oh, that's only a cow." said Timmy. "I will go and beg a little milk."

They were just setting off down the path, when Cock Robin flew down.

"Hide!" shouted Johnny, in fright.

"It's only my friend Cock Robin saying hello. Come along, Johnny, we haven't got all day."

"Whatever is that fearful racket?" said Johnny Town-mouse.

"That's only the lawn-mower," said Timmy. "Now we can fetch some fresh grass clippings to make up your bed."

Johnny waited while Timmy went to fetch the milk and the fresh grass. When he returned, it began to rain. "Oh! My tail is getting all wet!" complained Johnny.

  "It's only a spring shower. Here, take this leaf and hold it over your head like this," said Timmy. "The rain will brighten up the flowers. Come along, Johnny."

"I am sure you will never want to live in town again," said Timmy Willie to Johnny Town-mouse.

But he did! He went back in the very next hamper of vegetables. He said it was too quiet.

Johnny got back safely to his town-house and his old friends.

As for the two bad mice, they were not so very naughty after all, because Tom Thumb paid for everything he broke. He found a crooked sixpence under the hearthrug; and upon Christmas Eve, he and Hunca Munca stuffed it into one of the stockings of Lucinda and Jane.

And very early every morning, Hunca Munca comes with her dustpan and broom to sweep the dollies' house!

But Timmy Willie stayed in the country and he never went to town again. One place suits one person, another place suits another person. For my part I prefer to live in the country, like Timmy Willie.

THE TALE OF
PIGLING BLAND

Once upon a time there was an old pig called Aunt Pettitoes.

She had a family of eight: four little girl pigs, called Cross-patch, Suck-suck, Yock-yock and Spot; and four little boy pigs, called Alexander, Pigling Bland, Chin-chin and Stumpy.

The eight little pigs were always hungry and had very good appetites.

'I do believe I can't be coping much longer with my unruly brood,' Aunt Pettitoes sighed. 'They are indeed becoming a burden and a worry. Good little Spot shall stay at home to do the housework, but the others must go.

'Pigling Bland, you must go to market. You too, Alexander.'

Aunt Pettitoes handed the two little pigs their licences permitting them to travel to market.

'Beware of hen roosts, bacon and eggs, and mind your Sunday clothes,' she warned. 'And remember, if you once cross the county boundary you cannot come back.

'Take these eight conversation peppermints, and do heed the moral sentiments on them and you'll come to no harm.'

Pigling Bland and Alexander set off for market.

Pigling Bland and Alexander trotted along steadily for a mile, when Alexander began to feel hungry. They sat down to eat.

Alexander gobbled up his dinner and then asked for one of Pigling's peppermints. Pigling Bland said he wished to save them and held them out of reach. Alexander jumped up to try to get one and they both tumbled down, papers flying out of their pockets.

'That's quite enough, Alexander,' reproved Pigling
Bland, picking up the licences. 'Come along, it is a
long way to market.'

241

The two little pigs trotted along together, singing:

'Tom, Tom, the piper's son, stole a pig and away he ran.'

'Oh!' Pigling Bland gasped suddenly and came to an abrupt halt.

242

'What's that, young sirs? Stole a pig? Where are your licences?' the policeman demanded.

Pigling Bland pulled out his and showed it to the policeman. Then Alexander, after fumbling, handed over a scrumpled piece of paper.

'What's this?' asked the policeman, '2½ oz. conversation sweeties at three farthings? This isn't a license!'

'But I had one,' answered Alexander. The policeman looked doubtful.

'It's not likely they let you start without one. I'm passing the farm—you may walk with me,' and he led Alexander away.

Pigling Bland continued on his way dejectedly.

'Oh, I cannot bear the thought of market. I
never wanted to go in the first place. All I ever wanted was to have a little
garden of my own and grow potatoes.'

Pigling pulled his coat tightly round his neck, and put his hands in his
pockets to warm them. 'What's this?' he wondered. 'Alexander's licence!'

He started to run back. 'Oh, Mr Policeman! I've found the licence!'

But Pigling Bland took several wrong
turns and very soon he was quite lost.
The wind whistled and the trees
creaked and Pigling began to feel
frightened.

'I can't find my way home!' Pigling
cried. 'Wherever can I be? I can go no
further tonight I fear. I must find
somewhere to rest for the night and
shelter from this wind.'

Then past the edge of the wood Pigling saw a small wooden hen house and crept inside.

He squeezed between two hens.

'Bacon and eggs! Bacon and eggs!' clucked the hens.

'It is only a hen house, but what can I do? I must leave no later than daybreak,' resolved Pigling, feeling rather alarmed. He curled up and fell fast asleep.

In less than an hour, the door creaked open. The bright light from a lantern shone into Pigling's face. It was the farmer, Mr Piperson.

'I need six of you fowl to take to market in the morning,' he whispered to himself, grabbing a hen roughly.

'Here's another!' said Mr Piperson, seizing Pigling by the scruff of the neck and dropping him into the hamper.

Then he dropped five more dirty, kicking, cackling hens upon the top of Pigling Bland.

Back at the farm kitchen, Mr Piperson lifted Pigling out of the hamper.

'I am but a poor little pig,' said Pigling, showing his empty pockets at the farmer's request.

'You'll stay for supper?' asked the farmer.

'Yes,' replied Pigling Bland nervously. 'Thank you kindly.'

Pigling Bland sat on a stool by the fire whilst Mr Piperson pulled off his boots and threw them to a corner. As they hit the wainscot there was a smothered noise.

'Shut up!' growled Mr Piperson to the noise.

Indeed, it seemed to Pigling that something at the further end of the kitchen was taking a suppressed interest in the cooking.

Mr Piperson poured out three platefuls of porridge: one for himself, one for Pigling and a *third*. Pigling ate his supper discreetly.

After supper Mr Piperson consulted an almanac and looked at Pigling. Then he prodded Pigling's ribs.

'It's too late in the season for curing bacon,' he muttered to himself.

Then he turned to Pigling. 'Oh, well, you may sleep on the rug,' he said.

'You'll likely be moving on again?' Mr Piperson asked Pigling Bland the next morning. Before Pigling could answer there was a whistle from outside. It was Mr Piperson's neighbour to take him to market.

'Now shut the door behind me,' he continued. 'And don't meddle with anything, mind, or I'll skin ye!' said Mr Piperson menacingly.

Back inside, Pigling finished off his breakfast and began to sing to himself. Suddenly a little smothered voice chimed in.

Pigling listened carefully and went round the kitchen searching for the voice. Then he came to a locked cupboard. He pushed a peppermint under the door. It was sucked in immediately.

'Ah ha,' said Pigling. 'Very interesting.' He pushed in his last six peppermints, and they were all sucked up.

'How's Mr Piggy-Wiggy, then?' asked Mr Piperson when he returned from market.

'I must admit to being a little hungry,' Pigling answered.

Mr Piperson prodded him in the ribs again. 'You feel nice and fat to me,' he said laughing. 'Well, then, I had better fix some supper for us.'

After supper, Mr Piperson went to bed and Pigling Bland sat by the fire, eating his porridge.

All at once a little voice spoke—'My name is Pig-wig. Make me some more porridge, please!'

'I'm Pigling Bland,' replied Pigling, rather startled. 'More porridge? Of course. How did you escape?'

'He forgot to lock the cupboard,' Pig-wig replied.

'How did you come here?' Pigling Bland continued, handing Pig-wig his porridge.

'Stolen,' replied Pig-wig with her mouth full.

'What for?' enquired Pigling; to which Pig-wig answered, 'Bacon, hams.'

Pigling wondered why Pig-wig didn't run away. But Pig-wig didn't seem to know her way home.

'I'm going to market,' Pigling said. 'I have two pig papers. I might take you to the bridge, if you have no objection.'

'How wonderfully kind!' exclaimed Pig-wig thankfully.

Pigling told Pig-wig all about market and how he would much rather have his own little garden.

'I love flowers!' Pig-wig exclaimed.

'Potatoes,' corrected Pigling.

Pig-wig started to sing and very soon she was fast asleep.

Early the next morning
Pigling tied up his little
bundle and woke Pig-wig.

'Come along, Pig-wig. It's
time for us to be on our way,'
he whispered.

'But it's so dark,' complained
Pig-wig.

'Come away,' urged Pigling.
'We will be able to see when
we get used to it!'

Pigling Bland and Pig-wig
slipped away hand in hand
across an untidy field to the
road.

Presently, Pig-wig turned to Pigling and asked, 'Why do you want to go to market, Pigling?'

'I don't want,' replied Pigling rather miserably, 'I want to grow potatoes.'

They continued along the lane, hiding behind a wall as they passed a ploughman in a nearby field.

But suddenly Pigling stopped. Slowly jogging up the road came the grocer's cart.

'Take that peppermint out of your mouth,' instructed Pigling, 'we may have to run. Don't say a word. Leave it to me.'

'Where are you two going?' demanded the grocer. 'Are you going to market?'

The two pigs nodded. The grocer laughed. 'I thought as much—it was yesterday. Show me your licences.'

The grocer looked at their licences.

'I'm not sure,' he said, looking suspiciously at Pig-wig. 'This here pig is a young lady pig.'

He consulted the 'Lost, Stolen or Strayed' section of his newspaper.

'Ten shillings reward,' he muttered and went off to consult the ploughman.

'Just you wait here,' he warned.

Pigling and Pig-wig waited for a moment—and then off they raced!

They ran down the hill till they came to the river. They reached the bridge and crossed it hand in hand.

'Freedom! Safety!' cried Pigling happily.

'You shall have your garden, full of potatoes,' said Pig-wig with delight.

'*And* pansies!' replied Pigling.

Then over the hills and far away,
Pig-wig danced with Pigling Bland.
As they danced they sang a tune:
 'Tom, Tom the piper's son,
 Stole a pig and away he ran
 And all the tune that he could play
 Was *over the hills and far away!'*

ABOUT
THE WORLD OF
PETER RABBIT
& FRIENDS™

The illustrations in this book are taken from
The World of Peter Rabbit & Friends, a series
of animated films made for television and
video. On the following pages you can find
out how Beatrix Potter's stories were
turned into films.

THE MAKING OF AN ANIMATED FILM

An animated film is made up of thousands of separate still pictures. Each picture is called a 'frame' and each frame shows a gradually different stage in a movement. Every frame is photographed in sequence and then speeded up to flash past your eyes. This is how Peter Rabbit made his way from book to screen.

This rough character model sheet shows Peter Rabbit from all angles

1. SCRIPT

An animated film begins with the writer. Although the stories already exist, the writer has to adapt the tales to make them suitable as films, bringing the characters alive. The script contains speech ('dialogue') and some camera instructions.

2. CHARACTER MODELS

Beatrix Potter's illustrations provide the starting point. Using these and photographs of real animals, rough sketches are produced from which 'character models' are developed.

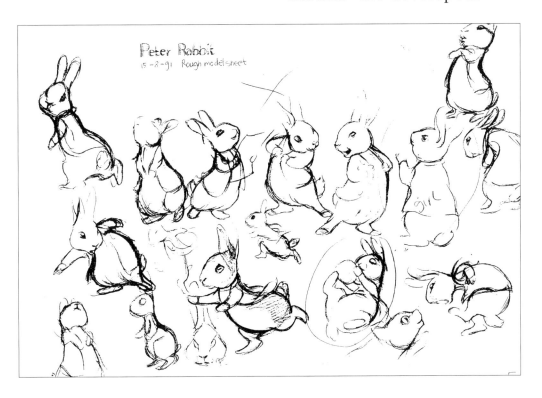

267

This story board gives an outline of one scene within the film

3. STORYBOARD

A storyboard looks rather like a comic strip and tells the key moments of the story frame by frame. Importantly, it enables the director and animators to visualise the story. The storyboard frames are often accompanied by a line of dialogue or some notes about the action.

4. SOUND TRACK

Before any film is shot the sound track is recorded. A sound track is made up of the voice track, the music track and the sound effects track – all recorded separately.

The voice track is recorded first.

Each noise will span a number of frames – this is recorded on a special document called a dopesheet. This will be used later by the animators to ensure that the mouth movements of the characters match up with what they are saying.

Meanwhile the composer writes music for the film, which is recorded on a music track. And finally, the sound effects are added.

5. THE ANIMATOR

The animator works on the drawings necessary to 'describe' the action. Using the script, character models, sound track and dopesheet, the animator begins by making 'key drawings' (the first and last drawings of a movement).

6. THE INBETWEENER

The additional drawings needed to smooth out the action between the key drawings are produced by an assistant animator, or 'inbetweener'. These line drawings are now filmed to test that the action works properly before moving into the next stage of production.

7. TRACE AND PAINT

Trace and paint artists trace the drawings from paper on to clear plastic sheets, called cels, and fill in the colour. The colour is painted on the *back* of the cels to make sure the colours are even and flat. The finishing touch is a special 'rendered layer' – this is a process which softens the outlines and adds textures with fine pencil and crayon giving the characters a three-dimensional effect.

Here, a cel on a background makes up the finished frame

8. BACKGROUNDS

The background artists have to produce backgrounds for every scene. The background is the painting on which a cel will be placed to create the complete scene. The artist refers closely to Beatrix Potter's drawings, the script and the storyboard.

9. FILMING

A person called the 'checker' makes sure that all the cels needed are in the correct order, and that all the backgrounds match with the proper scenes. The cameraman then photographs the cels in sequence.

The cameraman also works out all the camera movements (for instance close-ups, zooms, or fades) guided by the animator's instructions on the dopesheet.

The film is processed and an extra copy is made. This is called a work print and is passed to the editors for editing, whilst the first 'master' copy of the film is kept safely.

10. THE EDITOR

The editor puts all the different scenes of the film into the right order. They snip off little pieces of scenes that are too long, or add footage if a scene is too short. They also match the sound track to the action. The master copy of the film is then cut carefully to match the edited version and printed together with the sound track to produce the final finished film!

The finished film. There are twenty-four illustrations per second of film

270